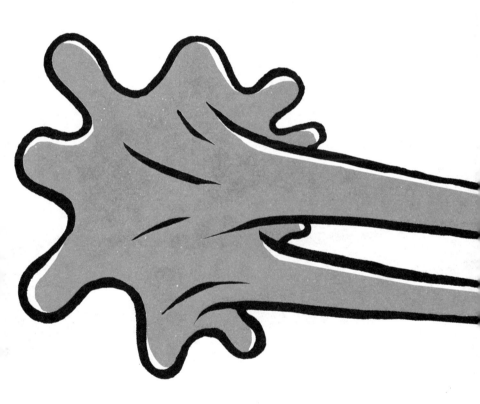

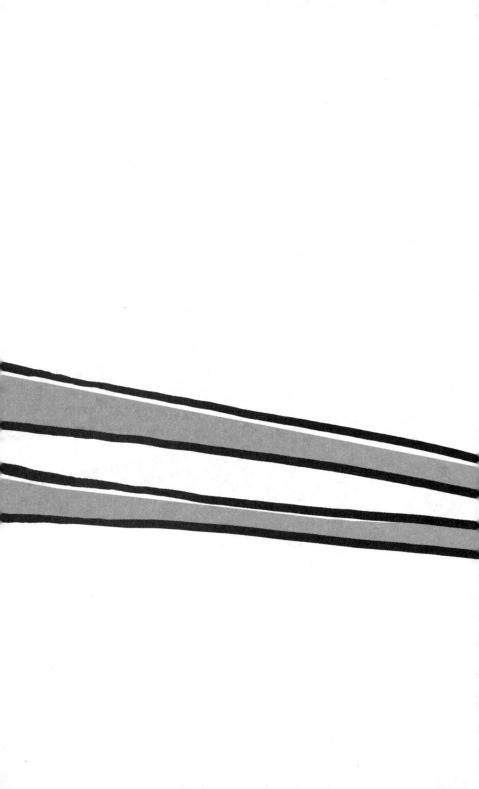

The GUMAZING GUM GIRL! GUM LUCK

RHODE MONTIJO

with Luke Reynolds

BOOK 2

DISNEP • HYPERION
LOS ANGELES   NEW YORK

Text and illustrations copyright © 2017 by Rhode Montijo

First Edition, June 2017
1 3 5 7 9 10 8 6 4 2
FAC-038091-17118

Printed in the United States of America
Designed by Maria Elias
This book is set in 14-pt. Grilled Cheese BTN Condensed / Fontbros.com

Library of Congress Cataloging-in-Publication Data

Names: Montijo, Rhode, author.
Title: Gum luck / Rhode Montijo with Luke Reynolds
Description: First edition. | Los Angeles : Disney-Hyperion, [2017] | Series:
    The gumazing gum girl! | Summary: Gabby Gomez keeps her Gum Girl heroics secret
from her parents, but there is a new villain in town and the city needs her to help.
Identifiers: LCCN 2016015026 | 9781423161172 (hardcover)
Subjects: | Bubble gum—Fiction. | Superheroes—Fiction. |
    Hispanic Americans—Fiction | Secrets—Fiction. |
Classification: LCC PZ7.M76885 Gu 2017 | DDC [Fic]—dc23
LC record available at 2016015026

Reinforced binding

Visit www.DisneyBooks.com

For my loves, Sylvia and baby Rode

CONTENTS

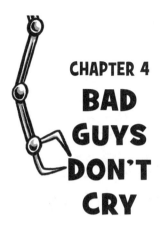
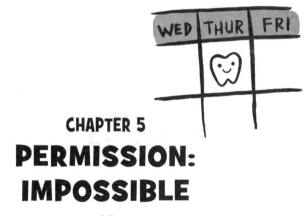

CHAPTER 1

STILL
STUCK

 **LAST TIME . . .** Gabby Gomez had done the impossible! She had saved a gigantic passenger plane with her bare— no, make that *gummy*—hands.

Now, just days after having one last piece of **MIGHTY-MEGA ULTRA-STRETCHY SUPER-DUPER EXTENDA-BUBBLE BUBBLE GUM,** Gabby was a hero.

Actually—thanks to an accidentally electrified popped bubble—she was a superhero.

She was **THE GUMAZING GUM GIRL!**

No one knew who Gum Girl was, though—not even Gabby's parents! So while Gum Girl's head was clouded by cheers, Gabby's heart was stretched to its limit. Yes, she was using her superpowers for good. But keeping a secret from her family made Gabby feel like less than a hero.

There was someone else who thought of Gabby Gomez as less than a hero, too. . . .

Deep in the shadows of an abandoned spatula warehouse, that *someone* was cooking up an evil plan. A mysterious masked man watched as a breaking news report glowed from his television. It was about Gum Girl.

Gum Girl! Sticking it to crime!

"My time of humiliation is over," the man
said. He picked up a rolling pin and hurled it
into a pile of spatulas. "Soon, I'll put my plan
into action."

His hat puffed with fury.

"I hate gum!" he yelled. Then he yelled it again . . .
and again. He didn't stop yelling until he kicked
an extra big, extra heavy, extra jumbo spatula.

It was extra painful.

The mysterious masked man hopped around the room pretending his big toe didn't hurt. *Bad guys don't feel pain!* But the throbbing only got worse when he landed right next to an extra tall, extra annoying stack of newspapers.

Smack on the top front page was a picture of GUM GIRL!

He grabbed the paper, crumpled it, and laughed an evil laugh. "Let's see how you handle something a little bit stickier!"

DUN! DUN! DUN!

CHAPTER 2

TO CHEW OR
NOT TO CHEW

Meanwhile, that same morning, Gabby was
struggling with the toughest decision of her entire
life. Deep in her stretched-out heart, she knew the
right thing to do was to tell her parents the truth.
It wouldn't be easy to admit she had broken the
"no gum" rule. And yes, she might have to give up
gum and Gum Girl forever. But it had to be done.

Then again, could Gabby really give up being
Gum Girl? *Should* she? Maybe, just maybe, she
could convince her parents it was all for the
greater good.

Her courage found, Gabby threw open her front
door and—

Gabby flew into her father's arms. "How was the convention?"

"Oh, you know the drill," Dr. Gomez said. "Toothbrushes, toothpaste, floss. Did you miss me?"

Gabby nodded with gusto.

"And since we're on the subject of teeth, let's have a look at my favorite set of chompers, *sí*?"

As a dentist, Dr. Gomez had a habit of checking teeth. You might think that after years of surprise checkups, Gabby would always be prepared for an inspection, but she rarely ever was.

"Open wide."

Gabby braced herself.

"Hmm . . . that's new," he muttered. "That could be a cavity. *No entiendo.* I don't understand. I thought your mom said no more gum."

Gabby grinned as best she could. One of her chompers *had* been hurting lately.

"Come by my office after school on Thursday," her dad said. "There's an open appointment, and I want to check out that tooth."

Just then, Gabby's mom walked in with Gabby's little brother, Rico. Everyone was there. *¡Perfecto!* This was her chance to tell the truth once and for all. Gabby opened her mouth to spill her Gum Girl secret—

"Gabby needs to come by the office, dear," her dad said. "Her tooth doesn't look good." Dr. Gomez looked at Gabby. "I'm very proud of you, though. It must have been hard to give up gum chewing. Just today, that new gum-chewing superhero was on TV."

"Gum Girl!" Rico flung his arms out far. "Sticking it to crime!" he yelled, repeating what he had heard on the news.

"*Aí, no.*" Dr. Gomez sighed. He knelt down next to Rico. "Stopping crime is good, *hijo*. But smothering teeth in sugar to do it is *not* so good, son."

Dr. Gomez turned to Gabby and Mrs. Gomez. "I can hear my patients now. They'll use this Gum Girl character as an excuse to chomp so much gum that they'll ruin their teeth. It's a dentist's worst nightmare!"

Gabby stood speechless.

"Honey," Mrs. Gomez said, "it isn't the kids' fault. What Gum Girl does is great. It's the gum that's bad. *Muy malo.* It's so, so bad."

Gabby's dad took a deep breath. "You're absolutely right, dear. Sorry, Rico. You too, Gabriella. But this Gum Girl really grinds my molars. You understand, right?"

All Gabby could do was shake her head. *How will I be a superhero if I stop chewing gum?* She slunk to her room. *And how will I ever tell my parents who I am?*

CHAPTER 3

SWEET
AND
SOUR

Gabby had no time to tackle her parent problem. Gum Girl was in high demand! The week was a roller coaster of spectacular superhero deeds. There were . . .

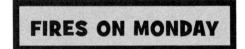

FIRES ON MONDAY

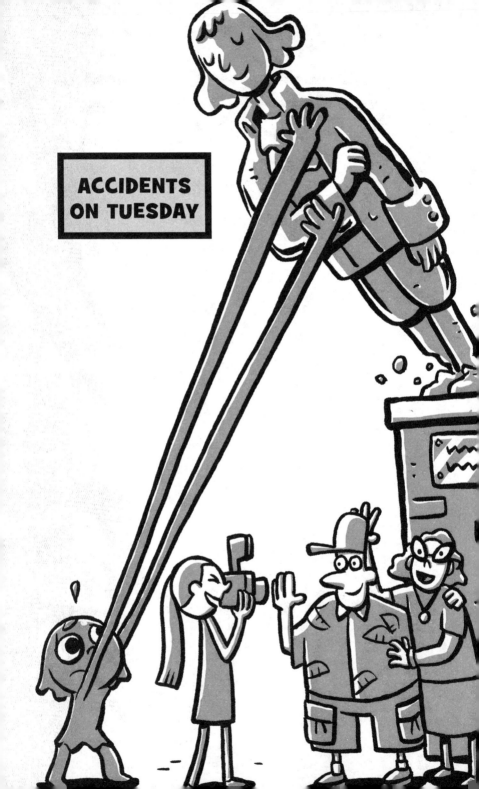

ACCIDENTS
ON TUESDAY

Gum Girl was saving the day right and left. She was on top of the world!

Gabby Gomez felt just the opposite, though. Her world was upside down.

Gabby's Thursday had started out well enough, as she continued her weeklong streak of hiding from mean old Natalie Gooch. That bully had been after her since the first grade!

Where could Gabby hide out today? Finally, she took a turn into the one place Natalie would never go: the library.

Wrong! Just when **Gabby** thought she was safe, there was Natalie.

Natalie sneered as all the coins from Gabby's pocket clattered on the floor. "Now pay up!"

"Pay up?" asked Gabby. "I don't owe you anything."

"How about your payment for me being KIND to you?" Natalie snorted.

Kind?! Natalie Gooch was NEVER kind. Natalie Gooch was a supreme bully. She was such an expert that other bullies looked up to her and even took notes on her bullying!

I should turn into Gum Girl and really stick it to Natalie, Gabby thought as she dangled there "donating" the rest of this week's lunch money. *THEN she would think twice before giving me a hard time!*

But deep down Gabby knew that going after Natalie as Gum Girl was not the right thing to do. Plus, it would give her secret identity away.

"That's a good Gassy." Mean Natalie Gooch dropped Gabby to the floor and quickly scooped up the money. "Looks like I'll have to be KIND to you more often."

Gabby glared at Natalie as she walked away. *It's time I teach that Natalie Gooch a lesson!* Gabby decided. She looked around and found one piece of gum. Bingo!

"You really shouldn't chew gum, you know. It's awfully bad for your teeth."

Gabby looked up and into the eyes of a boy she'd never seen at school before.

"Hi! The name's **Ravi Rodriguez.**" He extended a hand.

"Gabby Gomez."

"Well, Gabby Gomez, can I help you up?"

Gabby looked at Ravi's hand. Then she looked at her own hand holding the piece of gum. Gabby popped up and stuffed the gum back into her pocket.

"You seem very familiar, Gabby Gomez. Have we met?"

"Met? Where would we have met?" She couldn't shake the feeling that they'd met before, too. Then it came to her in a flash. *FLIGHT 808!* Gabby—er, Gum Girl—had managed to rescue the plane by reattaching its broken wing using gum! Ravi was the young reporter who had asked her about school and her age!

"Nope!" Gabby said. "We definitely haven't met before. Sorry. Got to go! I'm late for class."

Gabby bolted toward Ms. Smoot's room.

"Well, nice meeting you, Gabby Gomez!" Ravi called after her. "Hope to see you around."

"Sure, okay!" Gabby called back. *Good grief! That was close! Can this morning get any worse?* Gabby wondered.

34

At the end of the day, there was *finally* some good news, which quickly became bad news. That's when Ms. Smoot reminded the class about Friday's field trip to the zoo.

"Now, class, some of you have not returned your permission slips yet. If you don't have them tomorrow, you will not be able to attend. Those who can't go will have a guest substitute teacher," Ms. Smoot said. "He specializes in animals, so tomorrow will be fun for everyone."

With all the rescuing and superhero antics, Gabby had forgotten all about her permission slip.

¡Ai, no!

Gabby *loved* animals. And nothing was going to keep her from going on that trip. Nothing! *¡Nada!*

CHAPTER 4

BAD GUYS DON'T CRY

ELSEWHERE . . . Back in the abandoned spatula factory, the mysterious man pushed a button on a large remote control.

It *fizzed* and lit up.

The man's voice echoed through the darkness. His face glowed from the machine. He pressed another button, and a robotic mixer arm *whirred*.

He pressed a third button, and the top *buzzed* and opened. The man began to climb up the machine, which looked a lot like a ROBOTIC SUIT!

BZZZZ!

But his leg got stuck in the giant mixer arm! He slipped and flipped upside down.

"No!" The robotic suit began to shimmy. And shake. "No! No!"

And then the entire machine began to fall, fall, fall! A loud *crash* echoed throughout the factory. From under a pile of glimmering spatulas, the mysterious masked man emerged.

Why is it so hard to be good at being bad? he thought. *My creation was almost perfect. And now this!* He felt like he could cry.

But bad guys don't cry! They get even!

Plus, there was no time to cry. He had work to do.

Flinging spatulas in every direction, the man picked up his tool belt and started repairing his robotic suit. It would be ready in time—it had to be. Gum Girl was becoming unstoppable!

CHAPTER 5

PERMISSION: IMPOSSIBLE

Gabby skipped into her house with only the zoo on her mind.

"Mami, could you sign this, *por favor?*" Gabby waved the sheet of paper at her mother. "It's for a class trip to the zoo tomorrow!"

Gabby started to dance around the room.

There'll be elephants . . .

She made a trunk with her arm.

And giraffes . . .

She stretched out her neck.

And MONKEYS! Oot oot!

Gabby scratched and did her best monkey.

Mrs. Gomez smiled at Gabby. "Okay, okay, *mi amor*. The zoo sounds fun. But aren't you forgetting something?"

Forgetting something . . . wait . . . it was THURSDAY! There was a sudden ache in her tooth. Her appointment! She forgot! Gabby's excitement vanished, and her stomach felt the same as when mean old Natalie Gooch held her upside down: achy and queasy.

Just then, the phone rang.

"It's for you, Gabriella," said her mom.

"*Mi corazón*, are you okay?" Dr. Gomez asked.

"*Claro que sí*, Papi," Gabby replied. "It's just that, well, I am so sorry that I forgot the appointment. There's this field trip to the zoo tomorrow . . . and the permission slip . . . and Ms. Smoot—"

"Whoa, whoa, whoa," her father said. "One thing at a time. So there's a field trip?"

"*Sí*. And if I don't get my permission slip signed I won't be able to go. I'm really sorry for missing the appointment, but can I please still go? I'll come to your office right after the field trip!"

Before Dr. Gomez could answer, Rico zoomed into the kitchen, arms out wide and covered in . . .

. . . GUM!

Rico must have found Gabby's secret stash of gum and chewed it ALL!

Mrs. Gomez scooped up Rico in her arms. "To the bath with you!" she said. "I hope you like peanut butter. It's the only thing that will unstick you!"

¡Aí, no!

GUM GIRL!
GUM GIRL!

¿Qué paso?

Sticking it to crime!

Later that night, Gabby sat on the edge of Rico's bed.

"Rico, I know you like Gum Girl, but you can't chew so much gum. You'll get in big trouble with Mami and Papi."

Rico's eyes were getting heavy. "But Gum Girl is so good! Gum Girl saves the day!"

Gabby squeezed Rico's hand. "*Sí*, well, er, Gum Girl does save the day but, ah . . ." She couldn't figure out how to put it. "Too much gum makes cavities. It's bad for our teeth. You understand?"

Rico nodded, but Gabby wondered if he was just falling asleep. She leaned in and gave her brother a hug good night. His hair still smelled like gum.

Back at the abandoned spatula factory, the mysterious masked man paced back and forth. Before him lay the blueprints for a genius criminal plot.

A truly evil plan!

By a truly **BAD** guy!

Who *really* never cried!

This time, the robotic suit would be ready, and once and for all, he would have his revenge on the thing he hated most: GUM.

The robotic suit glowed and *whirred*. With the press of a button, the mixer arm rose and spun with great force and speed.

"Yes! It is finally ready!" The man cackled as the robotic arm swung just a little too close to his large chef's hat.

The mixer ground to a halt. Bits and pieces of hat fluttered to the floor.

"My time of humiliation is OVER!" the man yelled. "No more!"

DUN! DUN! DUN!

CHAPTER 6

CAR
TROUBLE

Friday was a great day for a trip to the zoo. Gabby was thrilled that her parents had signed her permission slip. She still felt confused about when to tell them the truth, but she didn't have time to think—

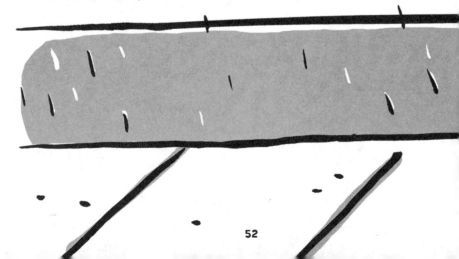

A tire blew out on a passing car! It went barreling past Gabby! Out of control, the car was heading right toward Gabby's school. . . .

Gabby reached into her pocket and pulled out her very last piece of gum. She raced after the car. It was only a few seconds away from smashing into the school! She tossed the gum into her mouth.

PLOP!

She chewed.

She blew.

FWOO

She popped into Gum Girl!

Thinking fast, Gum Girl rolled herself into a superstrong gum tire.

The car skidded to a sticky halt.

Gum Girl checked to make sure everyone was okay, then sprinted to school. Just before entering, Gum Girl grabbed her handy peanut-butter jar from her backpack and turned back into Gabby Gomez.

She took a few deep breaths.

Ms. Smoot was collecting permission slips for the zoo as Gabby arrived in class. "Your slip, Ms. Gomez?"

"Oh, yes!" Gabby smiled. "I've got it right . . . um . . . right here."

Gabby's permission slip was stuck shut.

She tried to open it carefully, but the paper was a gloppy, gooey mess.

No . . .

Gabby looked down at the floor as she handed the gummy slip to Ms. Smoot.

"I'm sorry, Gabriella, but this is illegible. You'll have to stay here with the others who can't make it."

But . . .

Defeated, Gabby stumbled over to her desk.

Gabby didn't have the energy to respond: she just slumped in her seat.

"Class, I think we have all the slips for those who will be attending the field trip today. For everyone else, please say hello to today's special substitute teacher, Mr. Hansen!"

CHAPTER 7

REVENGE IS SWEET

Deep in the abandoned spatula factory, trouble was heating up. "They said I was a bad chef before. Well, now I will show them all exactly how **BAD I** really can be!"

A show called *World's Silliest Videos* played in the background. A single clip looped over and over. It was of a chef tripping and falling during the Great Cake Competition.

His entire cake flew up in the air and then splattered everywhere. The audience erupted with laughter.

"No more!" the man shouted. "They say revenge is sweet, so it's time to get baking!"

The mysterious masked man rose from his chair and smashed the television set off its stand.

The video stopped. *Whirring* and *buzzing* and *beeping* filled the air as the man turned on his massive robotic suit.

This time, he climbed up a ladder next to the suit and got inside. He spun his gadgets and checked his power levels. The *handy* cake beaters sped in lightning-fast circles.

The doors to the warehouse opened. The giant machine *clunked* and *clattered* out of the spatula factory and into the world.

DUN! DUN! DUN!

CHAPTER 8

GOING
BANANAS

BACK AT SCHOOL . . . Gabby
struggled to stay awake as Mr. Hansen wrapped
up his lesson. "So, as you can see, class,
that's why hamsters are like mini lions. It's
a good thing this one is securely caged!"
Mr. Hansen chuckled.

"Have a good day. Remember that Ms. Smoot will be back on Monday."

Gabby bolted ahead.

Thank goodness that's done! Seeing how much food Mr. Hansen's hamster could stuff in its cheeks was no trip to the zoo. Even though she was glad school was over, Gabby wasn't thrilled about where she had to go next: her dad's office.

I just need to tell him the truth, Gabby reminded herself. It wouldn't be easy—especially with this hurting tooth! If it was a cavity, it was only going to make the truth even worse.

Gabby was a few minutes away from her father's office when she noticed something strange.

She blinked her eyes. Then she rubbed her eyes. Gabby shook her head from side to side. She couldn't believe what she was seeing.

Gabby pulled a slimy banana peel off her face just as shouts called out in the distance.

The voices came closer and
the commotion grew bigger
until—

A mob scrambled Gabby's way. They were Gabby's classmates!

GABBY, RUN!

Malik, Maria, what's going on?!

"Animals . . . animals on the loose!" yelled the panicked students.

Gabby reached for her pocket to find . . . *¡NADA!* She had chewed her last piece of gum that morning. *Oh, well,* Gabby thought. *They're just monkeys, right?*

Gabby knew she had to help—even though Natalie was the world's MEANEST bully. She didn't deserve to be pounced on by a runaway rhino, did she?

Gabby checked her pocket one more time. Still nothing.

CHAPTER 9

RHI-NO-
YOU-
DON'T!

"HEEEEEELP!"

Gabby panicked as she tried to think of a way to stop the raging rhino. A corner store across the street caught her eye—there was a **gumball machine** out front.

Gabby sprinted across the street.

PERFECT!

The machine was filled with Galactic Grape. Gabby gagged. *Not only is it the world's worst flavor,* Gabby thought, *it's also the STICKIEST gum ever created.* But a rhino rescue couldn't wait!

Gabby searched for change.

¡Aí, no!

But the very person Gabby was trying to save had stolen all her money!

Gabby frantically began shaking the gumball machine. **"PLEASE** give me a piece!" she begged.

Suddenly, a single grape gumball popped out of the machine and rolled away.

Boing!

Gabby dashed after the gumball.

YOINK!

Not only was **Gabby** now arguing with a monkey, but her last hope of helping Natalie was getting chewed up in front of her very eyes.

PTOOH!

Gabby pulled the super-sticky, gloppy, monkey-chewed gum from her face.

Gabby shivered.

She closed her eyes and put the whole monkey-chewed mess into her mouth.

"Everyone is distracted by the zoo chaos. They'll never guess that I unlocked all the cages! Who's laughing *now*?!"

The robot lurched forward.

Time to make a **CASH WITHDRAWAL!**

BACK TO THE CHASE

Gum Girl swung toward Natalie and the rhino.

She noticed that her whole body had turned Galactic Grape purple!

I just have to get right over the rhino and try to contain it somehow, Gabby thought as she positioned herself.

"Gum Girl, you did it!" cheered the crowd. Cameras flashed and news crews began to roll in.

ZZZIP!

One young reporter broke through the crowd. "Ravi Rodriguez here, student reporter." It was that kid from the library.

Gum Girl smiled as Ravi fired off questions:

"How did you appear so fast?"

"Who are you?"

"Where did you come from?"

"Why are you now purple instead of pink?"

"Do you attend school?"

"Uh . . ." Gabby was stuck. Fortunately, she was saved in the unlikeliest of ways: by mean old . . . Natalie Gooch!

The bully burst through the thronging reporters and hugged Gum Girl tightly.

"You saved my life!" Natalie said as Gum Girl peeled away the Galactic Grape sticking them together.

Before Gum Girl could speak, an alert blared out from a police officer's walkie-talkie:

Bank robbery in progress downtown!

Gabby was saved by the need to save! She breathed a sigh of relief as she called out to Ravi, Natalie, and the others, "Uh, sorry, guys, but there's more work to be done!"

"Wait, Gum Girl, any last words?" Ravi asked.

"Um . . . chew your food!" she said with an awkward smile. Everyone stared in confusion as Gum Girl sped away.

Gotta go . . .

ZOO

Chew your food? Oh man, that was terrible, she thought as she swung downtown. *Those reporters make me too nervous!* Below her, a swarm of police cars was rushing in the same direction.

CHAPTER 10

COOKING UP EVIL

Gum Girl swooped from building to building to . . .
a giant claw!

Towering above the city skyline, the huge robot carried an **ENTIRE** bank under one arm.

The robot pulled Gum Girl closer. She could see that there was someone inside the robot, controlling it with buttons and levers.

"Robo Chef! For years I trained to be the best
pastry chef in the world," he explained.

"So why did you turn yourself into a giant
robot, and why are you terrorizing the town, and
why are you holding me in your claw?" Gabby
asked frantically, stalling as she looked for a way
to escape.

"Why, you ask? I'll tell you why."

Robo Chef pulled the robotic claw toward his control-panel window. "I *was* the best in the world! I was in the finals of the Great Cake Competition. It was my finest hour. But then, as I approached the podium with my brilliant cake, I stepped on something. I fell! And my beloved delightfully-fluffy-yet-perfectly-springy, cream-filled creation splattered everywhere!"

Robo Chef's arms shook with anger. "Everyone laughed. And then the video spread like frosting. It even won on *World's Silliest Videos*!"

Gum Girl wondered if Robo Chef was about to cry.

People across the globe laughed at me—even my own mother!

"From that day forward I stopped baking cakes and started cooking up evil! Now I am Robo Chef! And THIS is Robo Chef's revenge!"

"You gave up too easy, mister! Everybody falls down sometimes—but what matters is whether or not you get back up. It's okay to cry about it and then try again!"

Even as Gum Girl said the words, Gabby wondered if *she* had really tried hard enough to be honest with her parents. Had she given up too easily, too?

Robo Chef drew Gum Girl closer, fuming with rage.

"But there's one more part to the story—the most important part. Do you know what made me trip and fall?" he asked.

Robo Chef answered his own question.

IT WAS GUM!

DUN! DUN! DUN!

CHAPTER II

ALL CHEWED UP

A huge crowd had gathered at the scene. Police cars and fire trucks and ambulances arrived, too.

Suddenly, Robo Chef bounced Gum Girl to the ground and turned on his supersized robotic mixer arm.

"Now I'm going to BEAT you up!" he yelled.

The hand lowered toward Gum Girl. The mixer revved faster and faster. . . .

Robo Chef twisted Gum Girl into a sticky mess! Then he peeled her from the wall, tossed her into his robot's mouth, and started chewing. The crowd gasped.

PTOOH!

Knowing he had **FINALLY** won his gummy revenge, Robo Chef spat her out.

Gum Girl plummeted
toward the ground.
She had to do
something, or else . . .

Thinking fast, she made
a **gum parachute** and
floated to safety.

WHOOSH!

On the ground, a crowd rushed toward her.

"Gum Girl, are you okay?" a police officer asked.

"*Sí* . . . yes . . . I mean . . . I think so." Gum Girl focused on Robo Chef. "*¡Ai, no!* He's escaping!"

I have to stop him!

Her gummy legs stretched into towers. Then she ran with all her gummy might.

Robo Chef raced down the street. "And this is only the start! Gum stopped me once, but NEVER AGAIN!"

An idea popped into Gabby's head. *That's it!* In a flash, she made a gum lasso.

She twirled the giant loop high in the air, ready to rope the bank.

Suddenly, a pop of pain surged through her tooth.

The pain zapped from her tooth throughout her mouth. Gum Girl's legs shrank and her lasso flopped. Her master plan was floundering.

Robo Chef laughed as he fled the scene.

This is what I get for all my gum chewing, Gum Girl thought. *If only I had been honest with my parents sooner, if only I had stopped chewing gum, if only . . .*

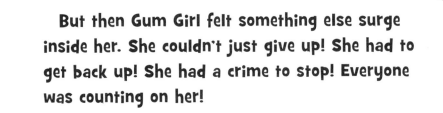

But then **Gum Girl** felt something else surge inside her. She couldn't just give up! She had to get back up! She had a crime to stop! Everyone was counting on her!

Suddenly, Gum Girl knew exactly what to do!

SHE STRETCHED HER EXTRA STICKY GALACTIC GRAPE ARMS.

SHE KICKED OUT HER EXTRA GOOEY GALACTIC GRAPE LEGS.

SHE TAPPED ON HER EXTRA BOUNCY GALACTIC GRAPE HEAD.

It was time for Plan B.

CHAPTER 12

PLAN B

Robo Chef was getting closer to the abandoned spatula factory. There, his arsenal of mechanized kitchen-appliance weapons awaited.

Gum Girl sprinted ahead faster than a speeding train!

Time for Plan B! She sped right past Robo Chef and rolled to the ground.

ZOOM!

She stood directly in Robo Chef's path!

"Ha-ha! You aren't the snappiest piece of gum, are you?!" Robo Chef said.

He lifted the massive mechanized foot and stomped right on Gum Girl!

A resounding gasp rose up from the crowd. What had Gum Girl done?! And WHY?!

Robo Chef took a mighty step toward the factory,
laughing. Until, suddenly, something went wrong.

It was **GUM GIRL**—
stuck to his foot!

The massive robot tripped, and the bank flew into the air.

No!

Robo Chef *whirred* to a stop. Some in the crowd began to cry. Had they lost their beloved superhero?

Then a tiny figure covered in spatulas
stretched out from the rubble.
"GUM GIRL!" the crowd cheered.

With her very last burst of energy, Gum Girl reached both her arms as far and as fast as she could. She caught the bank an inch away from the ground!

Police swarmed the scene and emerged
with a little man in handcuffs.
Robo Chef was no more.

Gum Girl listened to everyone calling out to her. She felt great pride and great shame. Gum Girl had defeated Robo Chef. But Gabby Gomez still held a big secret (and a cavity).

"Ravi Rodriguez here. Gum Girl, you just saved the day again. What do you have to say to your fans?"

"Kids, make sure to brush your teeth!"

Gum Girl smiled, stretched out one long gummy arm, and swung off into the sunset.

In the streaked sky, a lone figure zipped toward home. But she stopped halfway back and changed direction. There was NO WAY Gabby Gomez was going to miss her appointment with her favorite dentist *again*.

She was determined to keep her word. And that included one other last bit of unfinished business: finally telling her parents the truth about her secret identity.

MEANWHILE Sitting in a room full of trophies, someone was watching the media go crazy for Gum Girl. Someone who sneered and said, "I deserve all of that attention! And I know just how to burst that Gum Girl's bubble."

DUN! DUN! DUN!